Monster Monday!

For Oscar and Harriet

Published by BBC Children's Books,
a division of BBC Enterprises Limited,
Woodlands, 80 Wood Lane, London W12 0TT
First published 1994

This edition published exclusively for School Book Fairs, 1994,
by arrangement with BBC Books

ISBN 0 563 40389 6

Typeset by BBC Children's Books
Printed and bound in Belgium
by Proost NV

Monster Monday!

Susanna Gretz

BBC CHILDREN'S BOOKS

Every Monday, George has to play at Lottie's.

"Lottie's mum and I have a lot of work to do,"
says George's mum, "so play nicely."
"Of course they will," says Lottie's mum.

"That's *my* drum," says Lottie.
"I had it first," says George.
"George," says his mum, "please let us get on with our work."

"You broke my drum!" yells Lottie.

"I never did," says George.

"You broke it," yells Lottie.

"Didn't!" yells George.

"I can't concentrate at all," grumbles his mum.

"I want to go home," cries George.

So they do.

But soon it's Monday again.
"You *will* let us do our work today, won't you George?"
says his mum.
"That's the wrong way to wear your hat," says Lottie.

"And that's the wrong way to spread jam . . .

and the wrong way to skip," she says.
"It's the *right* way," says George.

"WRONG!" yells Lottie.
"RIGHT!" yells George.

"You've broken my toenail,"
cries George.
"I never," says Lottie.
"Did," cries George.
"I can't hear myself think," grumbles his mum.
"I want to go home," cries George.

So they do.

But soon it's Monday again.
"We'll be finished working very soon," says George's mum,
"so play nicely."

"Boys can't use face paints," says Lottie.

"They can too," says George.

"Can't," says Lottie. "Face paints are for girls."

"You look silly," says George.

"You look disgusting," says Lottie.

"I hate you, Lottie," yells George.
"Merciful monsters!" says his mum.
"We'll just have to go home . . ."

So they do.

But soon it's Monday again.

"You'd better play nicely, George," says his mum.

"Remember what happened last time."

"And the time before that," says George.

"And before that," says Lottie.

"You said I look disgusting," says George.
"I didn't," says Lottie.
"Did," says George.
It looks like another Monster Monday . . .

. . . but this time, George's mum pays no attention.
"Don't bother me now, George," she says.

George goes off in a huff.
So does Lottie.
"I'm not playing with *you*," she says.
But their mums don't even hear them.

Meanwhile, George gets busy on his own.
"What are you doing?" asks Lottie.
George doesn't answer.
"What are you doing, George?"
she asks again, creeping forward.

"George," says Lottie, "*look* at me!"
George still doesn't answer.

"I've got some blankets we could use," says Lottie.
"OK," says George, "there's still a lot of work to do."

"George, dear," calls his mum, "it's time to go home."
"I don't want to go home," says George,
"We're building a cave," says Lottie.
"A deep, dark cave in the forest," says George.

"A deep, dark, disgusting cave," says Lottie.
"Disgusting!" says George.
"That's nice," says his mum, "but come along now."

"NO!" yells George.
"Now don't behave like a little monster," says his mum,
"we'll be back next Monday."

"Next Monday is special," says Lottie's mum.
"It's Monster Monday!" says Lottie.

And it was.

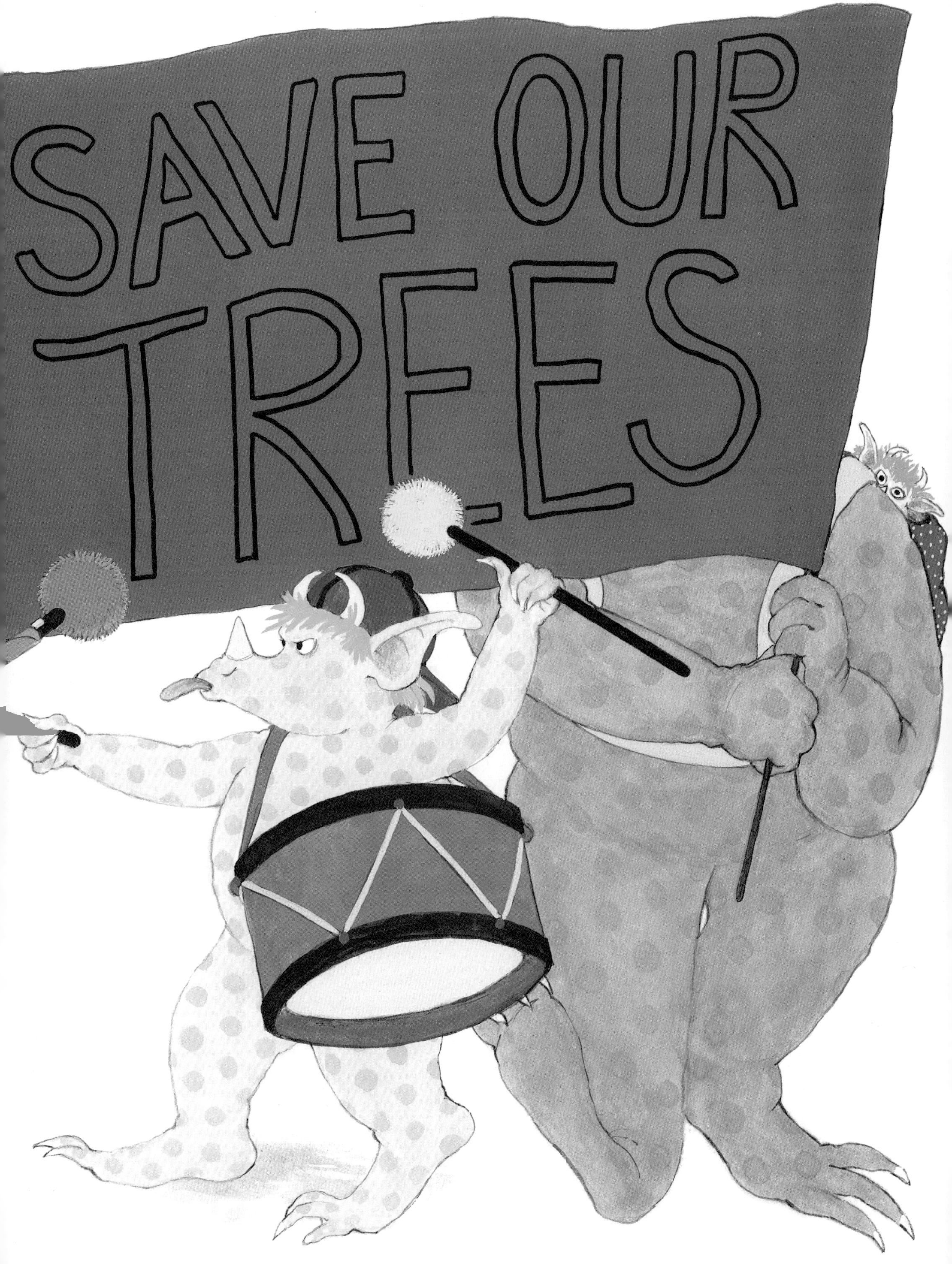
SAVE OUR
TREES